S0-BSM-332

Investigate

Settlements and Cities

Neil Morris

Heinemann Library
Chicago, Illinois

www.heinemannraintree.com
Visit our website to find out
more information about
Heinemann-Raintree books.

To order:

☎ Phone 888-454-2279

💻 Visit www.heinemannraintree.com
to browse our catalog and order online.

© 2010 Heinemann Library
an imprint of Capstone Global Library, LLC
Chicago, Illinois

All rights reserved. No part of this publication may be reproduced
or transmitted in any form or by any means, electronic or
mechanical, including photocopying, recording, taping, or any
information storage and retrieval system, without permission in
writing from the publisher.

Edited by Siân Smith, Rebecca Rissman, and Charlotte Guillain
Designed by Joanna Hinton-Malivoire
Original illustrations © Capstone Global Library
Picture research by Elizabeth Alexander and Sally Cole
Originated by Modern Age Repro House Ltd
Printed and bound in China by Leo Paper Group

14 13 12 11
10 9 8 7 6 5 4 3 2

Library of Congress Cataloging-in-Publication Data
Morris, Neil, 1946-
  Settlements and cities / Neil Morris.
    p. cm. – (Investigate geography)
  Includes bibliographical references and index.
  ISBN 978-1-4329-3472-9 (hc) – ISBN 978-1-4329-3480-4 (pb) 1.
Cities and towns–Juvenile literature. I. Title.
  HT152.M68 2009
  307.76–dc22
                        2009011046

Acknowledgements
We would like to thank the following for permission to
reproduce photographs: Corbis pp. **11** (© Geo Graphic Photo/
Amanaimages), **12** (© Bruce Connolly), **26** (© Wolfgang Kaehler);
Getty Images pp. **4** (Ron & Patty Thomas/Taxi), **18** (Pigeon
Productions SA/Riser), **22** (Keren Su/The Image Bank), **24** (Paul
Chesley/Stone), **25** (Barnabas Kindersley/Dorling Kindersley), **29**
(Robert Cameron/Stone); Photolibrary pp. **5** (Parent Parent/RESO),
7 (Bruno Morandi/Age Fotostock), **9** (Ken Gillham/Robert Harding
Travel), **10** (Ritterbach Ritterbach/F1 Online), **15** (Fraser Hall/
Robert Harding Travel), **16** (Liane Cary/Age Fotostock), **17** (LWA/
Dann Tardif), **21** (Imagesource), **23** (Gonzalo Azumendi/Age
Fotostock), **28** (Corbis); Shutterstock pp. **6** (© Fedor Selivanov),
13 (© Glenda M. Powers), **14** (© ExaMedia Photography), **27**
(© Keith Levit).

Cover photograph of an elevated view of Whitby, North Yorkshire,
UK reproduced with permission of Getty Images/Peter Adams/The
Image Bank.

Every effort has been made to contact copyright holders of any
material reproduced in this book. Any omissions will be rectified in
subsequent printings if notice is given to the publisher.

Contents

Some words are shown in bold, **like this**. You can find out what they mean by looking in the glossary.

What Is a Settlement?

A settlement is a place where people settle to live. Some settlements are home to many people. Others are very small.

⬆ This farmhouse is a settlement all by itself.

Many settlements were built next to a river, where there is fresh water.

Some settlements are new. Others are hundreds of years old. In a settlement, people can work, play, and share **services**, such as hospitals and schools, with each other.

5

Some settlements are made up of a small group of houses. Small settlements are sometimes called villages.

⬇ This village is high up in the mountains.

6

Homes in villages can be made of different things. Builders use materials that come from their local area. Here are some common building materials:

➠ wood

➠ stone

➠ brick

➠ dried mud

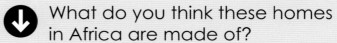 What do you think these homes in Africa are made of?

Towns and Cities

Over hundreds of years some settlements grow to become towns. The biggest settlements are called cities.

➡️ A tiny settlement can grow into a village, then into a town.

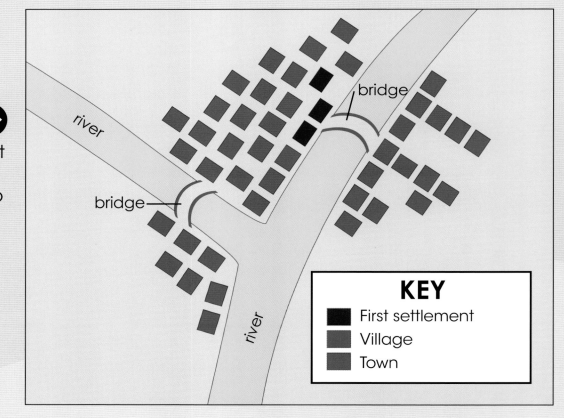

river

bridge

bridge

river

KEY
- ■ First settlement
- ■ Village
- ■ Town

Q What do people do at a street market?

? CLUE

- Why do people bring money to a market?

9

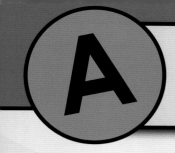
People buy and sell things at a market.

Many old towns have a market square. This is where farmers used to bring their food to sell. People still have **market days** in towns. Today, most town and city people buy their food in supermarkets.

10

The world's biggest cities have millions of people.

skyscraper

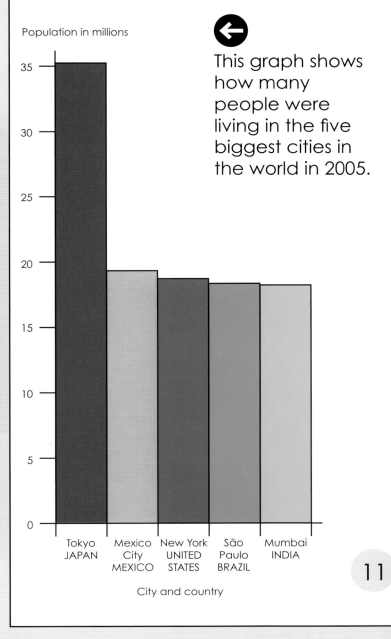

Population in millions

This graph shows how many people were living in the five biggest cities in the world in 2005.

Tokyo JAPAN	35
Mexico City MEXICO	19
New York UNITED STATES	18
São Paulo BRAZIL	18
Mumbai INDIA	18

City and country

Tokyo is the capital of Japan. It is the world's largest city.

Homes and businesses

apartment

house

Towns and cities are full of houses that people live in. Some people live in apartments in large buildings.

Q Where are these people having their **picnic**?

? **CLUES**

- It is a large open space.
- It has lots of grass and trees.
- There are play areas.

13

They are having their **picnic** in a park.

Parks are open spaces where people can enjoy themselves. They are like large gardens. In towns and 14 cities, people go to parks to get fresh air and relax. Parks usually have playgrounds where children can have fun.

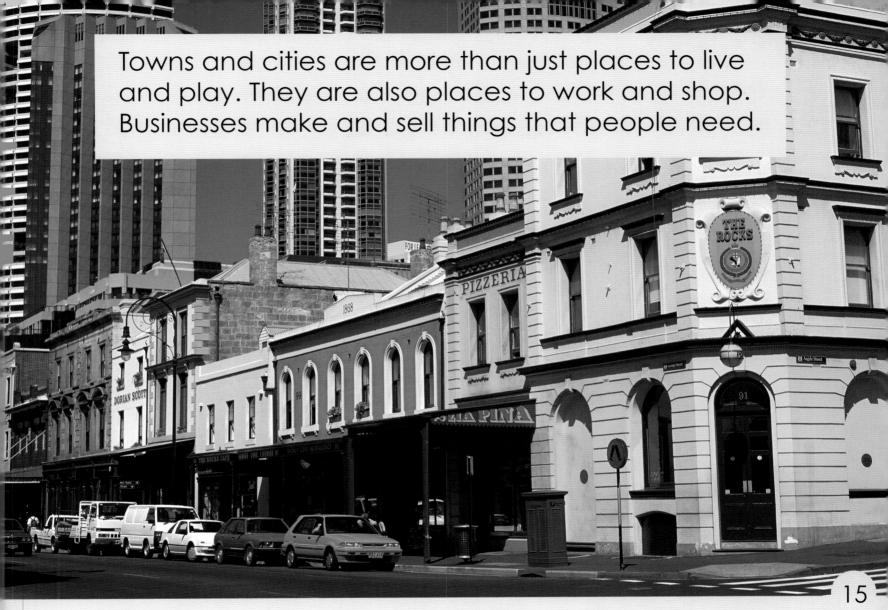

Towns and cities are more than just places to live and play. They are also places to work and shop. Businesses make and sell things that people need.

⬆ A city street has many different kinds of buildings.

Services

Villages, towns, and cities have schools, hospitals, and other **services**. The people who live there share these services.

All these services help people:
- fire stations
- hospitals
- libraries
- police stations
- post offices
- schools

Q Where does this person work?

CLUES

- She helps people if they are ill or injured.
- She helps people in an emergency.

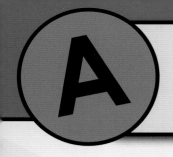

This doctor works in a hospital.

Local doctors have their own **clinic**, where people can go if they feel sick. The doctor may send them to hospital, where they can have special treatment.

18

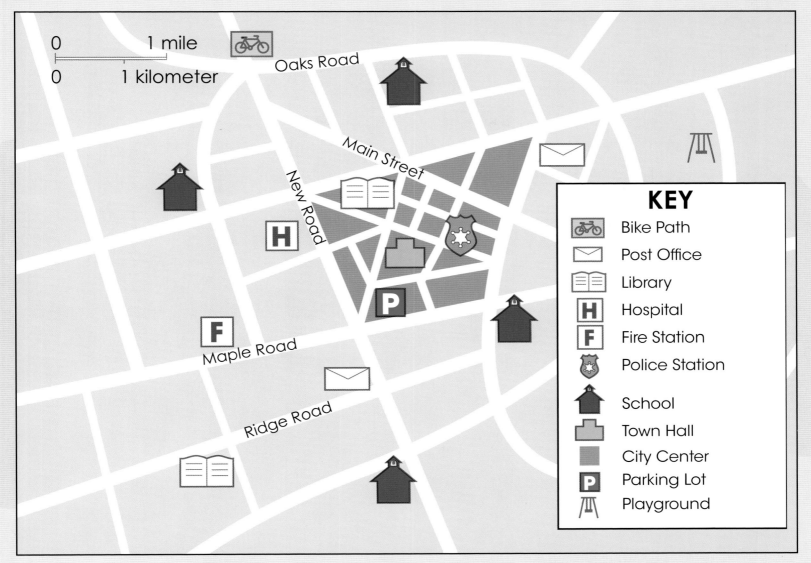

KEY

🚲	Bike Path
✉	Post Office
📖	Library
H	Hospital
F	Fire Station
🛡	Police Station
🏠	School
	Town Hall
	City Center
P	Parking Lot
🛝	Playground

Oaks Road

Main Street

New Road

Maple Road

Ridge Road

This map shows some of the different **services** in a town. Can you find the police station? Where would you go to send a letter?

Getting Around

Towns and cities have many roads and trains. They make it easy for people to get from one place to another. Roads and trains also link different places to each other.

This map shows the train and bus routes in a town.

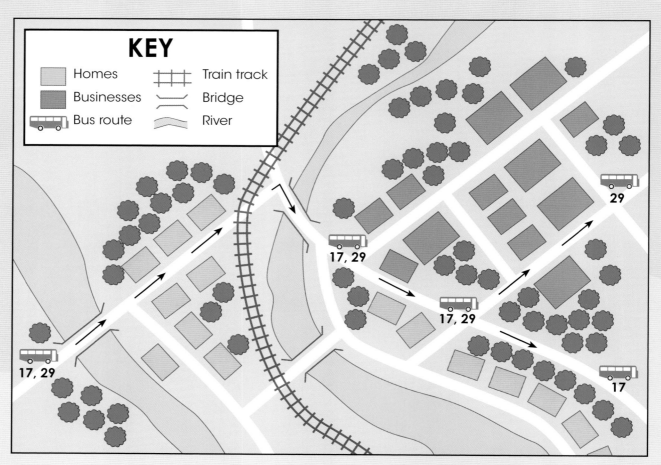

Q Which kind of transportation does not need fuel?

CLUE
- Human muscles do the work.

21

A Bicycles do not need fuel. Cycling is good for the environment because bikes use muscle power instead of fuel, so they save energy. Bikes do not **pollute** the air.

↑ Cycling is a good way to exercise.

People can also travel by public transportation. They might take a bus, a tram, a train, or a riverboat.

⬆ This **monorail** train is in Sydney, Australia. It is called a monorail because it runs on a single track.

23

Around the World

Towns and cities **vary** a lot in different parts of the world. A city in a hot place may be very different from one in a cold place. Towns and cities can also vary because people are either rich or poor.

⬆ This **shanty town** is in a poor district of Ho Chi Minh City, in Vietnam.

Q Do you think this settlement is in Africa or North America?

? **CLUES**

- Much of Africa is hot.

- Parts of North America can be very cold in the winter.

25

This is the town of Iqaluit, in Canada, part of North America.

People live different lives in different parts of the world. In northern Canada, many people travel around on **snowmobiles**.

snowmobile

Changes

Settlements change over time. Some small settlements grow into big towns or large cities.

 The city of Detroit, Michigan, grew into a city because of factories making cars.

People first lived in Paris, France thousands of years ago. At first it was a small settlement on the banks and islands of the Seine River. Today it is home to millions of people.

↑ This island in Paris was the city's first settlement.

Checklist

A settlement is a place where people live.

Some settlements are very old. Others are new. Settlements change over time.

Some settlements grow into larger towns and cities.

Cities are the largest settlements. A big city, such as London or New York City, is home to millions of people.

Settlements **vary** in different parts of the world. This is sometimes because of differences in the temperature and the weather that places usually get. Also, people have more money in some places than in others.

Glossary

clinic office where a doctor sees and treats patients

market day day of the week when a market is usually held

monorail train that runs on a single track

picnic meal that is eaten outdoors

pollute damage with harmful substances

services buses, trains, police, post offices, and other systems that provide people with what they need

shanty town settlement of poorly made shacks

snowmobile vehicle like a motorcycle for travelling on snow

vary to be different or change

Index